YOU BE THE

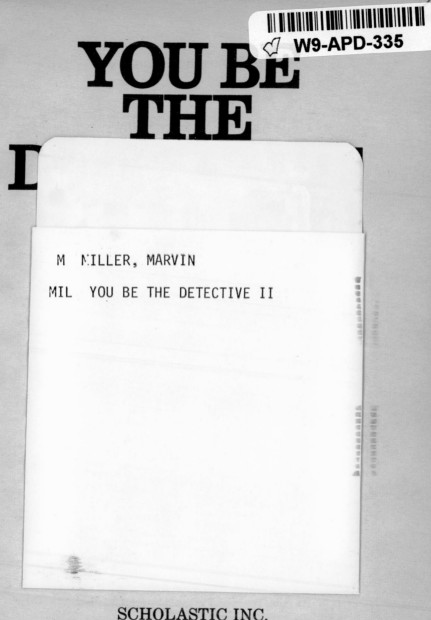

M MILLER, MARVIN

MIL   YOU BE THE DETECTIVE II

SCHOLASTIC INC.

New York   Toronto   London   Auckland   Sydney

For Randy and Audrey

Also by Marvin Miller:

YOU BE THE JURY
YOU BE THE JURY: COURTROOM II
YOU BE THE JURY: COURTROOM III
YOU BE THE JURY: COURTROOM IV
YOU BE THE DETECTIVE
WHO DUNNIT?

ISBN 0-590-45690-3

Copyright © 1992 by Marvin Miller.
All rights reserved. Published by Scholastic Inc.

12 11 10 9 8 7 6 5 4 3   4 5 6 7/9

Printed in the U.S.A.   40

First Scholastic printing, November 1992

CONTENTS

Welcome to Your New Job!

Welcome to the Bureau of Investigation. My name is Detective Alexander Riddle. As you know, this is my last day on the job. You will be my replacement.

I was a detective here for ten years, ever since I got out of law school. It's a good place to work. Chief Anvil is a tough but fair boss. But I decided that being a detective was not what I wanted to do in life, so I went back to school — to be an artist.

When I left the Bureau, Chief Anvil asked me to come back and help out during vacations and whenever I had extra time. I'm glad to do it.

Now I am turning my latest batch of files over to you. As you will see, I do my best thinking with a pencil and a drawing pad in my hands. For every case, I have sketched a drawing of the scene of the crime. There are often clues at the scene of a crime that a sharp eye can detect. Take a good look at the drawing and read my report of the case.

At the end of each case you will find another drawing. This drawing shows my sketch that solves the mystery. You will notice that I have cut this drawing into pieces and rearranged the pieces.

I have done this for two reasons.

First, you will have a chance to check my report and come to your own conclusion about the case. Then you can check your solution with mine by cutting out the puzzle pieces and putting my drawing back together again. (If you're having trouble putting the puzzle together, the number on the back of each piece will help you find the correct order. If you can't wait to do the puzzle, you can also find my written solution at the end of each case.)

Second, Chief Anvil is a puzzle fan. He loves putting together jigsaw puzzles. When I found this out, I decided to always give him the solutions to my cases as jigsaw puzzles. This way he could put them together for himself.

Well, I see it's getting late. Gosh, I'll miss this place. Here are my files. Good luck! I'm headed back to art school.

You be the detective!

The Case of
the Missing Guest

On May 15, I was at my desk at headquarters doodling on my sketch pad, when a phone call came in.

"Alexander Riddle?" The voice sounded familiar. "This is Dottie Warner."

I caught my breath. It was Mrs. W. — my fifth-grade teacher! I remembered her right away.

"Alexander, I haven't spoken with you in years," she continued, "but I need your help. Remember that motel I bought? Well, my last guest disappeared. I think he may have done something awful. He didn't pay his bill, either. Can you help me find him?"

"I remember the place. I'll leave right now," I said. "But . . . call me Alex."

A half an hour later, I nosed my car into a parking space under the big neon sign at Dottie's Motor Court.

Mrs. W. had purchased Dottie's Motor Court, planning for her retirement. She had expected she would need some extra income. Now, with the help of her young clerk, she rented rooms to travelers who could not afford something more expensive downtown.

"No time for the tour, Alex," she said. With her dog, Buster, at her side, she led me straight to the second floor.

"The guest said his name was Marlo," she explained. "He asked for a room with a high ceiling and brought an enormous trunk with him. It shook the steps as he dragged it upstairs. Everything seemed very suspicious."

"Tell me about him."

"Well, for one thing he spoke in a deep, controlled voice. Rather unusual. Anyhow, I left soon after he arrived. I was headed to the county fair.

"When I came back, Buster and I took a look around to check that all was well. When I passed room 23, something was wrong. I heard two voices.

"I recognized the deeper voice. It belonged to

4

Marlo. I'd never heard the other voice before. It was very high-pitched and sounded like no one I had ever heard. Very strange. At least twice, Marlo called this other person 'Billie.'

"Moments later, the voices disappeared. It was so quiet I could hear the chimes in the library. Next came a tremendous crash. Glass breaking. Hard objects falling. It startled Buster.

"Then I heard Marlo's voice again — an angry voice. Buster tugged at me. Then I heard the other voice again. Soon, it sounded like an argument. The voices became louder and louder."

"You didn't call for help."

"I didn't need help. I pounded on the door a few times to get some quiet for my other guests. But as suddenly as the argument had started, it stopped again. Silence again. No voices at all."

I shook my head. What dark secret did room 23 have hidden behind its wooden door?

When she had heard sounds of someone moving the trunk, Mrs. W. had decided to retreat with Buster to room 24 across the hall. She peeked through the keyhole. Soon, the door to 23 had opened.

"The trunk came out with him — *clunk* — over the threshold," Mrs. W. explained. "Then *ca-clunk, ca-clunk, ca-clunk* down the steps. I heard a car start, and he was gone."

"Did Billie come out with him?" I asked.

"No," replied Mrs. W., "and I don't think he's still in the room. Marlo must have shoved him in the trunk."

"Let's have a look."

As Mrs. W. swung open the unlocked door to room 23, I gave a shiver. I expected to see blood. But I was surprised. Room 23 was a bright room with a very high ceiling. A shattered skylight marked its exact center.

"What a room."

"I charge a bit extra for this one. Most people don't seem to mind. Of course, we know now why Marlo didn't mind. He wasn't going to pay his bill."

"He left quite a mess, too," I observed.

Broken glass from the skylight littered the floor and the bed.

I noticed that Buster seemed very interested in something under the bed. He began to sniff vigorously. But he wouldn't leave Mrs. W.'s side. She stopped beside the bed. Under her right foot lay a piece of clothing.

"And this. What is this?"

She stooped down and pulled out what seemed to be a bunched-up sweater or jacket.

"It looks small," she said, holding it up by the shoulders for me to see.

6

"Ruffles, too," she said, fingering the shoulders of the jacket. To me it looked handmade. Embroidery ran up and down the sides. Could it fit a small child? Barely. It also had a long slit down the back. This puzzled me greatly. I decided to make a sketch.

When I laid the jacket on the bed, Buster wouldn't let it alone.

"Did Marlo have a dog with him?" I asked.

"Only working dogs are allowed here," said Mrs. W. "Like Buster. I make it a practice not to allow any guests with pets. A sign in the office says so quite clearly."

"This looks to me like a jacket for a small dog," I told her. "Maybe a dachshund? The slit in the back might have fit around a leash."

"Buster would have let me know if a dog were on the property. Wouldn't you, Buster?"

At these words, Buster barked.

I continued my inspection of the room.

On the table I found four large dinner plates stacked neatly. Nearby lay five large, sharp butcher knives.

"Looks like Marlo had dinner planned, too. I wonder a bit about his choice of silverware, though." As I explained what I saw, Mrs. W. became very quiet.

"My guests know that I allow no food in my rooms. Do you see blood?"

"Nothing. Not a trace. No food, either."

I picked up a knife with my handkerchief. It was perfectly clean, and very shiny.

I felt relieved, but also puzzled. Why were there plates and knives, but no forks? Nothing added

9

up. Marlo had been in such a hurry that he hadn't bothered to clean up, and had left his own property behind.

And why the huge trunk? Could it really have held a person inside? Would Marlo have been strong enough to haul it downstairs?

"You are certain this 'Billie' wasn't a child?" I asked.

She seemed to be thinking. "I'm certain."

I held up the jacket one last time. Could it belong to a monkey? Could Marlo be an organ grinder? Of course not; monkeys don't speak.

I asked Mrs. W. to wait downstairs, and I started to draw. It all seems rather puzzling, I said to myself as I sketched.

A dog jacket? Knives without forks? Nothing seemed to make sense.

Suddenly, my face broke into a broad smile. I looked at my new drawing, then I cut it up and put it in my sketch pad. After a quick visit to the roof, I got a working description of Marlo from the clerk. I knew exactly where to find him.

Chief Anvil was certain to find this case quite entertaining. Besides, he's known all along that I was no dummy.

4

 8

 2

 9

 14

 10

 1

 15

 12

 7

 6

 11

 13

 5

 3

FINAL REPORT TO THE CHIEF

I had plenty of facts to juggle for this case. But the important clues came from the careful eavesdropping of Mrs. W., my "earwitness."

Marlo had come to town for the county fair. His trade was show business. His act included juggling. Marlo was also a ventriloquist. The second voice Mrs. W. heard was Marlo practicing his act!

"Billie" was Marlo's talking dummy. Billie's embroidered jacket had a slit in the back that fit Marlo's hand. This allowed Marlo to work the mechanism that opened and closed Billie's mouth.

Marlo took room 23 so he could practice his juggling before the show. The high ceiling gave him room to juggle the knives and plates he used in his act. He was working with the heavy dinner plates when he accidentally threw one too high. He caught and stacked the four plates that fell back into his hands. But number five sailed right through the skylight. I found it later on the roof, in two pieces. After the accident, Marlo left fast. He couldn't afford to pay for the damages.

Based on Dottie's description, Sergeant Emerson caught Marlo in the middle of his dummy act at the county fair.

— CASE CLOSED —

The Case of
the Country Club Code

Around three o'clock one summer afternoon, I was leaving Headquarters for the weekend when the phone rang. The caller asked for me.

I sighed and dropped my bags.

"Detective Alexander Riddle? This is Glenn Par at Glendale Country Club. I didn't call to sell you a membership, but you can have one for free if you can help me. My club is being vandalized. Could we meet . . . here, and talk about it?"

I glanced at my watch. "I'll be there as soon as I can, Mr. Par."

14

Twenty minutes after Par's call, I turned onto Tee-Off Drive. The sign for Glendale Country Club was impossible to miss, even with all the graffiti on it. I tried to make out what the graffiti said. "This place stinks!" That's what was written. Clearly, the club was having problems.

On the way to the clubhouse, I counted two dozen tennis courts and three pools, but only four people. The place looked deserted.

As I parked my car, a small single-engined plane flew low overhead.

Inside the club's office, Glenn Par looked worried.

"We have lost fifteen members this month," he told me. "If we lose any more, I will have to close down for good. Everyone knows we have a problem. But I suspect that someone in the club has been helping the vandals."

Par took me outside and showed me the swimming pools. The water in one pool had turned a sickly green color, another an inky black, the third a milky white. I wondered if this was someone's idea of a joke.

"When did these crimes happen?"

"All in the past two weeks, all at night."

"Do you have any idea of what is going on?"

"Well, Detective, just before this began, I received a call from a person who would not identify himself," Par said. "He asked if the club was for sale. When I told him no, he offered me $500,000."

"Without telling you who he was?"

"Crazy, right? Besides, we're worth close to $3.5 million. But even with the tennis courts, three pools, the golf course, and clubhouse, the land is worth more as open fields."

"To whom?"

"To our neighbor, Sterling Airport. You must have heard a plane as you drove in. The noise never stops. What's worse, the airport has plans to expand. Our clubhouse sits 200 yards from the end of their runway."

"Have you spoken with them?"

"The people at Sterling Airport swear they don't know anything about it."

"Do any of your members use the airport?"

"We have two amateur pilots on our Board of Directors. Both Babs Pringle and Skye Smith are fine pilots. They both use Sterling Airport."

Finally, we were getting somewhere. Two suspects. A motive. An inside job, perhaps.

I quizzed Par on night security. Here's what he told me: "Four guards watch the club at all times. Every day I meet with the Board of Directors. We keep changing the guards' schedule so no one else can figure out where they will be. But the vandals seem to know which areas of the club are unguarded," explained Par.

I decided to take a closer look around outside, with Par following behind.

I found two doors in the outside wall of the club that faced Sterling Airport, both locked. One exited from the sport shop. The other exited from the squash courts. There was also a small window. It opened easily from the outside.

Glenn Par told me the window belonged to the laundry room.

"But the laundry room door opens right next to the front guard desk of the main club room," he said firmly. "If someone came in the laundry room window and walked into the club, the guard would see him or her."

As we walked toward the laundry room window, I noticed it was streaked with a thin white coat of soap. Suddenly I stopped.

"Look!" I said to Par. "When you stand over here, you can see strange marks on the window."

We looked closely.

"It's a message," I told him. "Someone wrote in the soap with a finger."

I quickly drew what I saw on the window. It looked like this.

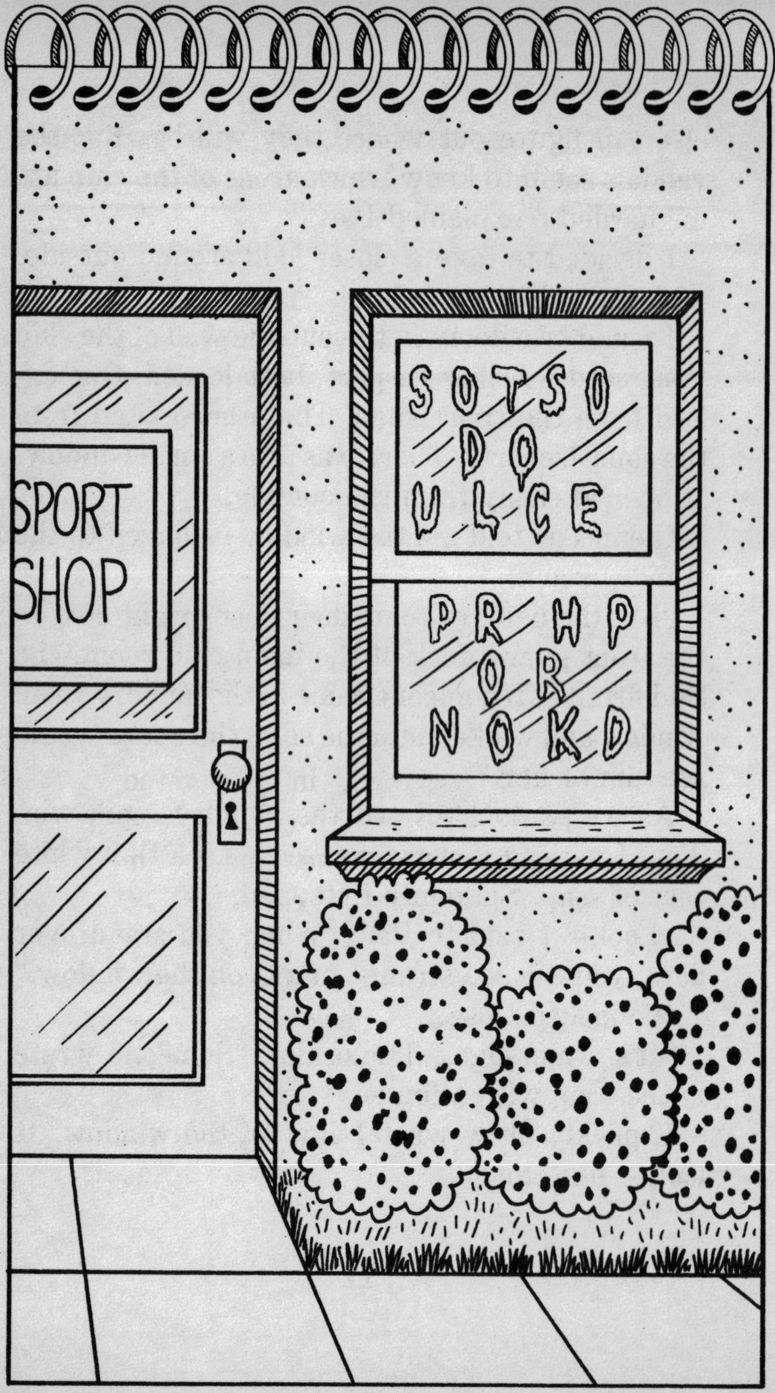
SPORT
SHOP
SOTSO
DO
ULCE
PRHP
OR
NOKD

Someone had taken care to write each letter very clearly. Unfortunately, the letters formed no complete words. I couldn't make sense of it. Then I smiled. Codes were my hobby.

I went back inside and took a comfortable seat in the lobby, while Par went to check on some things.

An hour later, I still had nothing. It looked like nonsense. I looked at my sketch and tried reading the letters backwards and forwards. The spacing of the letters bothered me. My brain felt scrambled. Perhaps it wasn't a code at all.

This was a tough one. Was someone who worked in the laundry room helping the vandals? Was it a guard? Then, why?

Then it hit me. My mind began to speed up. If someone had walked right into the laundry room the way I had, that person could have left messages for the vandals on the window almost anytime. I knew I was getting close.

Par returned.

"Does anyone other than the workers have keys to the laundry room?" I asked.

"Not really," said Par, scratching his head. "Only the guards. And of course the members of the Board of Directors have pass keys to anywhere in the club."

Maybe it was Smith or Pringle, I thought. We

already knew that they flew in and out of Sterling Airport regularly. Perhaps they wanted a bigger airport, too. Perhaps they were even willing to give up their tennis games to expand the airport.

The night guard would have caught the vandals if they had entered the club the same way, time after time. The code on the window must have told the vandals where to enter the club without being seen by a guard. But how did they make sense of it? Somehow, I had to break the window code.

I closed my eyes and began to daydream. I remembered a summer job I took one hot, muggy summer. I painted houses. Windows were easily the worse part of it.

That was it. So easy! Quickly, I redrew the window and the letters on it. That was it! Now I knew what the window code message said.

Before leaving, I cut up the drawing and put the pieces in my briefcase for Chief Anvil. I told Par where to wait for the vandals as they tried to enter the clubhouse. When I showed him my drawing, he smiled and nodded.

I figured Anvil would be happy to let me take off an extra day or so for solving this one. It was an open-and-shut case.

9 15 8

1 3 13

2 11 10

6 4 12

7 5 14

FINAL REPORT
TO THE CHIEF

Clearly, someone connected with the airport wanted the Glendale Country Club to go out of business.

That someone turned out to be Skye Smith, as the vandals quickly confessed when Glenn Par and his guards caught them. Sometimes Smith left a door in the clubhouse open. Sometimes he had his hired vandals enter through an open window. But he always used the laundry room window to signal them. The vandals didn't need to know any codes.

Every night when Smith left the club, he wrote a new message on the soaped-up window. When the vandals arrived, they quickly opened the window, pushing up the carefully spaced letters on the bottom windowpane into place over the letters on the upper one, making a complete message. The message told them the easiest way to sneak into the club. It said, "SPORT SHOP DOOR UN-LOCKED."

— CASE CLOSED —

The Case of
the Narrow Escape

On a rainy August 4, I worked late. It was around seven P.M. when I finally called it a day.

Outside of Headquarters, a dense fog lay over everything. Would my drive home turn out to be as tiresome as the rest of my day? I decided to head over to Don's Pork Barrel, one of my favorite restaurants. There, I could wait out the fog.

On the way to Don's, a small blue pickup truck came barreling out of the fog behind me. I swerved to the shoulder of the road just in time to avoid being hit. The truck went screeching around a curve and sped off. Its two red taillights disappeared into the fog.

I waited while two motorcycles passed before I pulled back onto the road. Now I felt more than tired. I was angry and hungry.

24

When I got to Don's, I saw a parking spot next to a blue pickup truck. As I pulled my car in, I looked the truck over carefully. It seemed bigger than the one that had almost hit me. But I didn't feel sure. I was suspicious, but I shrugged it off.

Inside the restaurant I sat down and ordered a big plate of chicken wings with a side of celery and extra blue cheese dressing.

Don's had a good crowd. Lots of people were enjoying themselves. But out of the corner of my eye, I saw two customers in some kind of hurry to leave. Suddenly, there was a big commotion. A waitress was running toward the kitchen, yelling.

"They didn't pay! They didn't pay!"

I threw my chicken wing down on my plate and joined the chase. Through the glass in the door I could see two red taillights speeding by toward the back of the parking lot. They're trapped, I thought to myself with satisfaction. The back of the parking lot ends in a brick wall.

Just as I had suspected, the pickup truck that had been parked next to my car was gone. I ran toward the back of the parking lot, but when I finally reached the wall, my eyes went wide. The truck had disappeared.

Quietly, a white figure came up behind me in

the dark. I turned. A long knife flashed at his side.

"Put the knife down, Benny." It was Benny the cook, wearing his kitchen whites. He had a flashlight in his other hand.

"Did you catch them?" Benny said.

I shook my head. Then I pointed to the flashlight. "May I borrow that?"

I inspected the brick wall at the back of the parking lot. On the other side of the wall was an open field that met the road further on. There was an opening in the wall — the only way out through the back of the lot. But it was much too narrow for a truck to fit through.

There could be only one answer.

The truck must have turned around and gone out the parking lot's front entrance. But why didn't I see it? I shook my head in bewilderment.

Walking back to the front door, I nearly tripped over a long board lying across the gravel. By chance, the light caught a pair of fresh tire tracks. I looked closer. If the truck had turned around, it would have driven over the board a second time. It would have made another pair of tire tracks on the board as it left — a total of four tire marks in all. I looked for more. Nothing.

I stared down in disbelief.

26

"I think we have a case of a vanishing truck," I joked to Benny. But I felt extremely puzzled.

I stopped at my car and pulled my sketchbook from the trunk. With the help of Benny's flashlight, I drew the scene at the back of the parking lot. It looked like this:

When I had finished, I checked again for tire tracks. But the gravel parking lot would tell no tales. Only the long board lying in the gravel had any evidence on it. That evidence left me even more puzzled. Then I noticed something new. The tire tracks on the board seemed quite far apart. How big a truck did I see?

I tried to picture the truck that almost hit me on the road. Then I looked back at the board. The distance between the tire tracks was much too far apart for a pickup truck. Maybe an 18-wheeler ran that wide, but these tire tracks didn't belong to an 18-wheeler.

I went back inside the restaurant and asked Don if he could describe the two men. He seemed uncertain, but he remembered that they both wore black leather jackets and boots.

I made a quick call to Headquarters and told them to be on the lookout for a blue pickup truck. There was nothing more for me to do, so I decided to return to my dinner.

How the truck left the parking lot without my seeing it was a mystery. So were those tire tracks. While I waited for Benny to reheat my wings, I took out my sketch pad and started to draw the opening in the rear wall again.

It was much too narrow for a pickup truck to drive through. But if the truck had turned around,

I would have seen its taillights. Even in the thick fog. How could the truck have gone out?

Don's description of the two men flashed through my mind. I began sketching as fast as I could think.

Suddenly it hit me like a ton of bricks. I stared at my drawing with satisfaction. It was the only way a single pair of tire tracks could have driven over the long board without turning around.

I telephoned Headquarters and told them my description was a mistake. This time I had the right one.

I finished my drawing and cut it into pieces. I knew Anvil would enjoy seeing how the clues finally fell into place one after the other.

MENU 10

MENU 13

 MENU 7

MENU 14

MENU 5

MENU 15

MENU 1

MENU 9

 MENU 3

MENU 6

MENU 11

MENU 8

 MENU 12

MENU 4

MENU 2

FINAL REPORT TO THE CHIEF

The end of this case showed me just how tired I had been. I had indeed parked next to the truck that almost hit me.

My mistake was to assume that it was the truck's lights that I saw. In fact, the culprits were both riding motorcycles! It was the red taillights of their two motorcycles that beamed through the fog. They escaped through the wall in the back of the parking lot, passing through the narrow opening single file.

A few miles down the road, Sergeant Phil DeCannon had pulled the men over, thanks to my call to Headquarters.

— CASE CLOSED —

The Case of
the Striped Pickpocket

On Saturday, June 24, I spent the morning at Balsam Lake. By eight-thirty, a crowd had gathered. Soon, a strange collection of boats lined the far shore. Then a megaphone blasted.

"Good morning. Welcome to Balsam Lake and the Second Annual 'Anything That Floats' Boat Race."

So much for peace and quiet, I thought.

Soon sailboats, kayaks, paddleboats, inner tubes, canoes, shells, and rafts made from every kind of scrap material covered the lake. I took out my sketch pad and started to draw a few.

Just then, two women walked by and blocked my view. One of them acted very upset. When I saw her showing the other an empty purse, I decided to introduce myself.

"Detective Alexander Riddle at your service," I said.

Mrs. Tiller and Mrs. Windlass told me they had come to watch the boat race. They were deciding upon a spot for viewing, when a man came up from behind and bumped Mrs. Tiller, knocking her down. By the time she was back on her feet, the man had walked away.

"He said he was sorry," explained Mrs. Windlass. "But he didn't seem to mean it. He just turned and left." Then Mrs. Tiller noticed that her purse was open. Several items were missing, and the man had robbed her of eight crisp ten-dollar bills.

When I asked for a description of the man, neither woman could tell me what his face looked like. They just hadn't seen it. But they both remembered quite clearly what he looked like from the back.

"He had a striped shirt and short brown hair," said Mrs. Windlass.

"Balding slightly," added Mrs. Tiller.

"Wait," said Mrs. Windlass. "I took a picture of the lake earlier with my instant camera. There were people in the picture."

She gave me the photo.

Mrs. Windlass didn't have a very steady hand when it came to taking pictures, but the two friends pointed to the same balding, brown-haired man in their photo.

I asked to borrow the photograph for a while. A few minutes later, I had reproduced the important details in a larger sketch. Here's what my Saturday morning pickpocket looked like:

The man appeared to be easily identifiable: brown hair, a striped shirt, and balding. He also appeared to have a large, old-fashioned mustache. If he were still working the crowd, I could find him.

I told Mrs. Windlass and Mrs. Tiller to meet me at the boathouse in an hour. I hoped to have a suspect by then. Suddenly, a loud shot rang out.

It was the starter pistol. The race had begun.

I walked behind an almost solid wall of spectators now lining the western shore of the lake. When I'd gone a quarter mile or so around, I spotted a man in a striped shirt.

I closed in quickly. I compared my sketch to the man's back. The fit seemed close enough to ask a few questions.

Cyrus Lugg said he was a boatbuilder. Though he didn't have an entry in the race, it interested him greatly.

What interested me was his mustache. It looked as if someone had drawn it on with a pencil. Whether or not it was real, it hardly matched the man in my sketch.

Lugg also seemed to have an alibi. He had just taken his first bite out of an unusual snack: a triple hot dog, wrapped in a sesame seed hamburger roll — hot dogs Balsam-Lake style. He must have just returned from the boathouse concession stand. He couldn't have committed the crime. He'd been too far away.

I thanked Cyrus Lugg, and resumed my search. Farther around the lake, I spotted another man in a striped shirt, standing by himself. He was facing me, so I circled around behind him. It looked like I had another suspect: brown hair and balding.

The suspect looked carefully groomed. His hair was perfect. His shoes shone with polish. But he didn't want to identify himself. That seemed suspicious enough. So I showed my badge. A quick inspection of his wallet turned up a name: Fester Fairweather. Mr. Fairweather's wallet contained about $150.

Considering how carefully he had dressed and groomed himself, the mess inside Fairweather's wallet was surprising. On one side of the billfold, ten and one-dollar bills in crisp singles lay perfectly arranged. The fronts of all the bills faced the same way. But folded in half in front of this money were eight crisp ten-dollar bills, some facing up, some facing down. That might be money belonging to Mrs. Tiller.

Fairweather wouldn't look me in the eye. Suddenly, I noticed something. He didn't have a mustache. The odds were that I wouldn't find another balding, brown-haired man in a striped shirt at the race today. Could the mustache have been a disguise?

I demanded that Fairweather empty his pockets. Maybe I'd find a fake mustache. But no luck. All he had was some gum and a ring of keys.

I was convinced Fairweather was the thief. He looked like the photograph from the back. And the eight crisp ten-dollar bills in his wallet were too much of a coincidence. But how could I prove it? He didn't have a mustache.

I took out my sketch pad and asked Fairweather to turn around. Reluctantly, he agreed.

I was about to sketch, when I glanced over at the lake.

A boy in a red canoe won the race by half a length. Behind him I saw Mrs. Tiller and Mrs. Windlass, standing on the far shore. Mrs. Windlass took a picture.

I watched them walk a few yards. Boats drifted about on the lake between us. Then an idea hit me as soon as my pencil hit the paper.

I quickly sketched Fairweather. First I drew him from one side. Below that drawing I drew a larger sketch directly from the back. Finally, I drew him from his other side.

Then I added some background details and circled the middle drawing.

There! I had the final proof that Fairweather

was the pickpocket in Mrs. Windlass' photograph.

"You can turn around now," I said to Fairweather. "I'm placing you under arrest for pickpocketing."

I cut the drawing up for the Chief, and put it in my sketchpad.

Anvil would thank me for this one. He'd know the thief was up a creek without a paddle. Maybe now he'd quit telling me not to make waves.

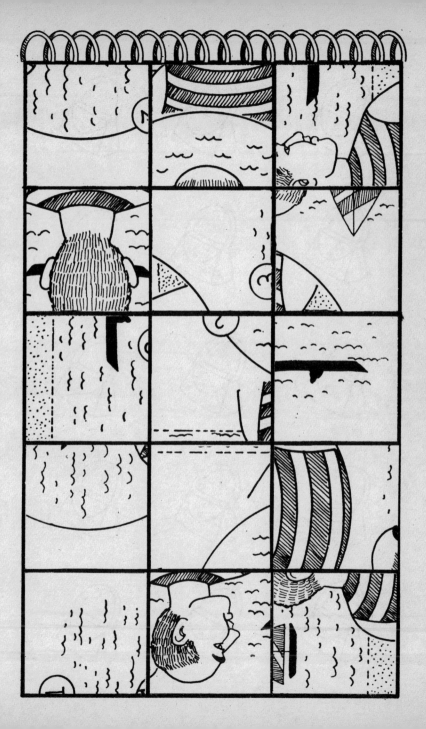

9

 5

 14

 8

 12

 10

 15

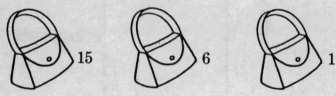 6

 1

 7

 4

 11

 3

 2

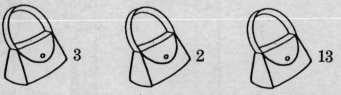 13

FINAL REPORT
TO THE CHIEF

I had my pickpocket, all right. His real name turned out to be Buster Mulruddy. Police in nearby Hillsville knew Buster very well.

Mrs. Windlass's photo had helped me find Mulruddy. But it had also confused me. With her unsteady hand, Mrs. Windlass took a blurred photo of Mulruddy's back. So what looked like the ends of a large, old-fashioned mustache were really the bow and stern of a canoe.

The camera caught the canoe at the exact moment its paddler had disappeared behind Mulruddy's head. The ends stuck out to the left and right of his head as he faced the lake. The blur made the upturned ends of the canoe look fuzzy, like a mustache.

When I had made my sketch, I drew the object behind Mulruddy to look even more like a mustache than it did in the photo. What else could it be? Now I knew.

— CASE CLOSED —

The Case of
the Leap Year Thief

On February 29, a call came into Headquarters from P. Jack Hilton, the wealthiest man in town. He wanted to talk to me.

I took a deep breath and picked up the phone. "Hello, Mr. Hilton. How can I help you?"

"Detective Riddle, I have a case for you. If you're interested, please meet me at my estate at 1 Hilltop Lane."

Hilton didn't need to say another word. I had already guessed what the case was about.

The papers had been full of stories about the Tripoli diamond Hilton had purchased recently. They said he paid $6 million for it. They also said he had had it made into an engagement ring that he planned to give to his fiancée as a surprise. Good luck, Mr. Hilton!

Of course, it hardly surprised me that a criminal or two might have read about the purchase and made different plans for the diamond.

"I'm on my way, Mr. Hilton," I told him.

Twelve minutes later, I made a right turn into Hilton's mile-long driveway and pulled up in front of his enormous house.

Hilton met me at the door.

"Detective Riddle, I presume." Then he whispered in a low voice, "Please come in and meet our suspects."

Hilton introduced me first to Mark Manx, an appraiser. Manx's business was to estimate the value of jewelry.

"And this is Joshua Creeper," said Hilton, nodding to a man in overalls. Creeper worked for Hilton as a gardener.

Then Hilton showed me the way upstairs. The two men followed. Outside his bedroom suite, Hilton told me his story. It seemed simple enough.

45

According to Hilton, only three people were on the property at the time of the crime: Manx, Creeper, and Hilton himself. That explained their introduction to me as suspects.

Since the purchase, Hilton had kept the famous ring in a secret safe in his bedroom. In late February, he decided to find an expert to tell him if the stone was really worth what he paid for it. He called Manx, and Manx agreed to do the work.

Manx lives three hundred miles away in Harrison. So Hilton offered to fly him to the estate for the day — in his private jet. But Manx refused. He insisted on driving. Because it was such a long ride, Hilton invited Manx to stay the night in the guest suite. Manx accepted.

That night was February 28. Manx worked very late, inspecting the valuable gem carefully. Finally, Manx finished, and Hilton returned his diamond to the safe. But because he was tired, Hilton forgot to spin the lock before going to bed.

At seven A.M. this morning, February 29, Creeper arrived as usual to tend plants in the greenhouse. Hilton left his house to go jogging soon after Creeper arrived, locking the door behind him. After three loops around his long driveway, Hilton returned to the house. He found his safe empty and his bedroom a mess.

Manx claimed that police sirens woke him up.

Creeper claimed that he had been in the greenhouse the whole time. He said he didn't have a key to Hilton's house, so he couldn't have gotten in anyway.

Hilton's safe lay hidden in the floor of his bedroom, built under some tiles near the fireplace. He had done the work himself. He said no one else knew exactly where the safe was. But somehow the thief found it.

"The police already dusted the room for fingerprints," Hilton added. "Nothing. Zilch."

I stepped into Hilton's bedroom to inspect the damage. What I saw astounded me.

Clothing from Hilton's four huge closets lay everywhere. The sheets had been torn off the mattresses of two beds. Parts of one mattress had been ripped open. Three pillows lay in a pile, spilling feathers over a chair and into a clump on the floor.

One detail particularly interested me. A bedroom window had been unlocked. It remained open about six inches. Through the window, I spotted a storage shed between Hilton's pool and the flower garden.

I asked Hilton about the window. Hilton said he hadn't opened it. He also suggested I speak with Joshua Creeper about the shed outside. Hilton didn't have a clue what might be inside it.

Creeper agreed to give me a tour. Inside the shed, Creeper kept tools and supplies for the garden and the pool. I spotted two pairs of gardening gloves. I also saw a ladder hanging from the ceiling. Was it tall enough to reach the open window? I decided to experiment.

I set the ladder against the house. It was impossible to keep steady as I climbed. Twice, I nearly fell as I tried to reach Hilton's windows. The soft dirt below wouldn't support the ladder's feet. One side or the other would sink into the dirt, tipping the ladder over. As it fell, the top of the ladder left a curved orange line on the side of the house. I looked for other marks on the house. But the ones I made were the first and only marks.

The thief had probably not used a ladder.

Back inside the house, I inspected the guest suite where Manx had slept. On the bed lay his open briefcase. It held papers related to his work, business cards, a magnifying glass, and a pair of white gloves. I also found a small picnic basket in the room. It contained some crumbs that looked like some rice and peas, perhaps leftovers from a lunch he had packed for the long drive. I borrowed one business card, for reference.

Then I returned to Hilton's bedroom. The scene looked so confusing, I decided to sketch.

As I worked, I thought about what I had

learned. Both suspects had driven to Hilton's property. Both had access to gloves, to hide fingerprints. If Creeper were telling the truth, Manx was the only one in the house at the time of the crime.

As I compared my sketch to the scene around me, I noticed a difference. I had missed a few feathers inside on the floor below the window, and a row of flower pots outside. Now my drawing looked like this:

I thought about the flowerpots. They would have made it difficult for a person to climb into or out of the window without knocking one over.

I thought about the feathers. They had probably come from one of the torn pillows. Most of these feathers lay on or beneath one chair. A breeze from the open window probably scattered the few remaining feathers on the floor.

But why would there be feathers below the window? A breeze coming through the window should have blown the feathers further into the room. This didn't make sense.

If only I could figure out what the thief had done with the ring, I'd be closer to knowing his identity. I'd already checked, and the ring wasn't in either Creeper's or Manx's car.

The diamond. The window. The feathers. Hilton. Creeper. Manx. My mind held onto each piece of the puzzle for a moment, and then let it go. As I thought, I fingered Manx's business card in my pocket. I began to imagine Manx finishing his lunch in the guest suite.

Then I snapped out of my daze. Something seemed fishy. Wouldn't a guest ask his host for something to eat if he were hungry? Why would Manx have brought the picnic basket inside at all?

All of a sudden, I had it — a very clever crime. Simple, but well planned. The thief could have been completely searched and the diamond ring never found.

I redrew the scene in Hilton's bedroom, adding a few details of my own. My fingers flew as I sketched. When I was done, I was sure I had the answer. I borrowed Hilton's phone and called the Harrison police. Then I cut up the drawing and put it in my briefcase.

The nightly news on every TV channel showed the thief in handcuffs at Headquarters with Chief Anvil. I knew that Anvil got the message right away, when he put my puzzle together. He obviously saw that this evidence was nothing to sneeze at.

5

 13

 1

 11

 3

 6

 10

 15

 2

 12

 14

 7

 4

 9

 8

FINAL REPORT TO THE CHIEF

The feathers by the window did not match the feathers from the pillows. The pillow feathers came from a goose. The feathers by the window came from a pigeon — a carrier pigeon. Manx's well-trained bird turned up that same afternoon, standing beside its cage on the roof of Manx's office in Harrison.

Manx brought the bird into Hilton's house hidden inside his picnic basket. He fed the bird peas and rice in preparation for its long flight. In the enormous house, Hilton didn't hear the bird cooing.

As a jewelry appraiser, Manx worked with wealthy customers all the time. Most of them kept their valuables in a safe. It was just a matter of finding Hilton's safe.

Manx's opportunity came when he heard his host leave the house. He raced upstairs with his gloves, a piece of ribbon, and the bird. Once he had found the safe, Manx quickly threaded a ribbon through the ring. He tied the ring around the bird's neck. Then he opened the window just wide enough to let out the bird. Then he fled back to the guest suite, to prepare his alibi.

— CASE CLOSED —

The Case of
the Missing Expert

I had just settled into a comfortable chair to watch the late news at home when the phone rang. Not Headquarters, I said to myself.

"I can't find my husband, Bill," the caller chirped. "I'm afraid he might be missing."

It was my neighbor, Betty Winter.

"I've called everywhere," she said in a small, anxious voice. "I'm really worried. I thought you might know where he is. I need your help, Alexander."

I barely knew my neighbor, Bill Winter. He seemed like a pleasant guy, although he was a bit of a know-it-all. I told Betty I'd be right over.

Two minutes later I stood in Betty's kitchen. My hair was soaking wet. The rain was coming down harder than I had thought.

Betty explained what had happened. She said that she and her husband had gone out to dinner at the mall. Then they rented two movies for their VCR.

Back at home, Betty dozed off halfway through *The Galloping Ghost and Other Football Greats.* She said she was half asleep when the phone rang.

"Bill answered the phone. All he said to me was, 'I'm going over to the Lanes', Betty.' When I was fully awake, he was gone."

"What woke you?"

"The phone rang again. Bill works for the highway department. They needed Bill to look at the condition of a bridge out on the interstate. They had to decide whether or not to reopen the bridge to traffic in this rain."

"Was that an unusual call for your husband?"

"Not at all. He gets them all the time, especially in bad weather. I told the highway people he was visiting our best friends, the Lanes. But when I called Greg and Rhonda Lane, he wasn't there. They didn't even expect him. I had assumed that's where he had gone. He had never arrived."

"We can drive the route you think he might have taken," I suggested. "But let me make sure I understand all of the facts. Was anything out of place after he left?"

"I don't think so. I found the VCR turned off, and the tape back in the box. He must have changed his shirt, too. He left the shirt he had been wearing on the bed. But he must have worn the same pants. He's never worn that pair to work before. Oh, his storage closet door was open, too."

"Let's take a look at it." Betty led me to the closet and left to get a drink of water. What I saw inside amazed me. It was a disorganized jumble of old golf clubs, dusty soccer balls, a broken vacuum cleaner, and old clothes piled from floor to ceiling. It was hard to imagine this clutter belonging to a self-proclaimed expert on everything, like Bill Winter.

I pulled out my pencil and sketch pad and started to record the scene for evidence.

Here's my sketch of the closet:

Betty returned while I was drawing.

"What a mess!" she exclaimed. "I had no idea he kept his closet this way! Bill never leaves his other things in such a state."

I knew something didn't fit.

When I asked Betty what Bill could have been looking for in such a hurry, she said she couldn't imagine. But there was an empty space on the floor smack in the middle of all the junk. Betty looked at it carefully and thought for a moment. She agreed that something might be missing, but she didn't know what it was.

"Tools?" I asked.

"No, he keeps everything for work in his car."

Our next discovery didn't help matters. Her husband's car was still in the garage. Betty turned a little red when she saw it. It still had his tools in it, too.

My neighbor's problem had just become a serious case. I suggested Betty call the highway patrol, local police, and highway department immediately. That gave me a few moments to think over the details of the case carefully.

I imagined Bill Winter changing his shirt. Where would he be going? I thought again about the closet. What would he take? That might depend upon where he went. I imagined someone picking him up in a car. There, I had no leads.

Betty had assumed Bill had gone to the Lanes' house. But now she didn't know who had telephoned Bill. I thought about his last words to her. He had said, "I'm going over to the Lanes." She was dozing. Maybe she didn't hear them correctly.

I pulled out the pencil and paper again. I began to rhyme words with "Lanes."

rains
panes
gains
canes

I filled each word into the rest of Bill's sentence, "I'm going over to the _____."

None of the rhymed words made sense.

Then another idea came to me. When Betty hung up, I asked her for the names of other friends whose names rhymed with "Lanes." Here are the names she gave me:

Bains
Kanes
Pains
Blaines
Zanes

I sent her back to the phone. She called each set of friends, one by one. She came back. Nothing. I was stumped.

I started doodling on my sketch pad to help clear my brain.

Suddenly, I got a new idea. That was it!

A strange call, a change of shirt, and something missing from the floor of Bill's storage closet. It all seemed to fit.

I turned to a blank page and quickly sketched where I thought Bill was. Then I showed it to Betty. She seemed surprised.

Betty called one more number. It confirmed my hunch. Betty looked embarrassed, but thankful, too.

I quickly cut up my new drawing and put it in my sketch pad.

Chief Anvil would really be impressed this time. Now he'd realize I was on the ball. I'd solved the case with time to spare.

11

 14

 2

 13

 5

 1

 15

 7

 10

 9

 3

 12

 4

 8

6

FINAL REPORT
TO THE CHIEF

Bill Winter had gone to the lanes — the bowling lanes. After his wife had dozed off, a friend called Bill on the phone. A member of their bowling team had come down with the flu. He asked if Bill could fill in just this one night. He'd pick him up as they'd have to hurry to get there on time.

Bill changed into his bowling shirt and dug his dusty old bowling ball out of the junk closet. Betty heard Bill say exactly where he was going. As he kissed her good-bye, he said, "I'm going over to the lanes."

— CASE CLOSED —

The Case of
the Stolen Idea

On December 30, a screaming man called Headquarters.

"I need sharpshooters! Helicopters!" he yelled. "I want to talk to the President."

I thought for a moment.

"I think you may have the wrong number, sir," I said.

The man told me not to hang up. He said he was Otto A. Osgood, the inventor. In a few moments, Mr. Osgood calmed down enough to tell me his problem.

He said he had misplaced something in his office.

"Or someone stole it," he said, heating up again. "Not just any piece of paper, mind you. A blueprint — a blueprint that could change the course of our country. On that blueprint was a design for an engine that burns water, instead of gasoline. Do you understand how important an invention like that could be?"

I decided not to answer the question. Instead, I suggested that I come right over. A theft of an idea was still a theft, after all — no matter how harebrained an idea it was.

It took seven minutes to reach Osgood Industries. The inventor's business was on the eighth floor of the Tuck Building. His three rented rooms — an office, a design lab, and a shop — had all the charm of a prison. An electric eye rang a loud bell when anyone walked in or out of the place. I counted four locks on each of the company's doors. For a moment I wondered if I would ever get in. Later, I wondered how I would ever get out.

I looked at my watch. At six-thirty P.M., the place seemed empty. Only three people remained: Osgood, his assistant Judson McLever, and Bertram P. Peck, a janitor hired by the owners.

Osgood led me into his private office, a hodgepodge of tables, lamps, drawings, clay models, and empty file cabinets. Osgood liked to leave his files on the floor.

Osgood's desktop stood in sharp contrast to the rest of his office. In fact, it looked spotlessly clean and perfectly organized. His phone sat on the right. His pencils, rulers, and staplers sat lined up perfectly in a neat row on the left.

Osgood pointed out the desk drawer where he had kept the blueprint. He said he had returned

the drawing to his desk at 4:30 P.M. He discovered it missing at 5:30 P.M. During that hour, no one had entered or exited Osgood Industries.

I decided to make a sketch of the office.

As I worked, I noticed that the windows had been cleaned recently. In fact, they were as spotless as the top of the desk.

"Who besides you has been in your office today?" I asked.

"These two gentlemen," said Osgood, motioning to McLever and Peck. "McLever is in and out of my office all day. Mr. Peck came in at about five o'clock. I left him alone in my office to clean it."

"It took me six minutes," Peck explained. "Mr. Osgood doesn't let me do more than clean his desk and the windows. I hate leaving this mess."

"The man fusses with my office," muttered Osgood. "He makes everything so neat. Even my desk doesn't look like it's mine."

"Has anyone left the office since four-thirty?" I asked Osgood again.

"No," he insisted. "Bells would have rung."

That settled it. The blueprint had to be in Osgood's office. I figured that whoever stole it planned to pick it up the next day, when he wouldn't be noticed.

I questioned Peck a bit. He said he had nothing to hide. He even offered to let me search him and his trash barrel. I couldn't tell if Peck was smarter than he seemed, or not.

I asked McLever to show me his desk. It was located in the design area. Peck had polished McLever's desktop with the same care he had used on Osgood's desk. But unlike his boss, McLever didn't seem to mind.

"He's something, isn't he?" said McLever, nodding toward Peck.

"It must help you stay organized," I said.

"I don't need to be organized," said McLever. "I have a photographic memory."

I raised an eyebrow.

"I could keep an office the way Osgood does," explained McLever. "But I still would never lose anything. I can always picture exactly where I left something, if I am the one to leave it."

"And when did you last work on the missing blueprint?"

McLever looked me straight in the eye. "I left it in Osgood's hands at 4:30 P.M. I saw him put it in his desk."

I thanked McLever and left to join Osgood in his office. I decided the time had come to be direct with him.

"How much do you know about McLever?" I asked him.

"McLever!" squealed Otto Osgood. "McLever

doesn't need to steal blueprints. I've given him a share of any profits we make from the engine. Besides, he doesn't need to steal a blueprint to steal the idea. He could take it to our competitors anytime. He has it all up here." Osgood tapped his forehead.

"Photographic memory," I said.

"It's quite remarkable," Osgood said. "Though not quite as remarkable as my engine."

I was about to call Headquarters. I would need some help searching the place. But something made me hesitate. I decided to look over my own drawing again. From my drawing, I could easily see where Peck had cleaned in Osgood's office: the windows, the desktop, and the wastebasket.

I carefully checked each place in turn — every drawer and file cabinet. I even checked the bottoms of the drawers in case the blueprint was taped there. No luck. With chicken wire covering the windows, the thief couldn't have thrown the blueprint to an accomplice below. After an hour of searching, I was running out of possibilities.

I looked at my watch. It was getting late. I glanced once more at my drawing.

The blueprint had to be in Osgood's office. But where?

The neat desk stood out in sharp contrast to Osgood's files cluttering the floor. Peck sure was a meticulous cleaner. Not one thing was out of place.

Suddenly, I had it — an almost perfect hiding place.

I turned to a blank page and began to draw. Now I was certain who the culprit was.

When I finished, I walked over to the hiding place that I had sketched.

There was the blueprint! I carefully removed it.

Then I cut up my drawing for Chief Anvil and put it in my sketch pad.

Five minutes later, I walked out of Osgood's office. We had caught the thief.

"Good luck with your engine, Mr. Osgood," I said, nodding.

"Call me Otto, Detective Riddle. And thank you for your help."

I could hardly wait for Anvil to figure this one out. It would be clear to him that I was really on a roll.

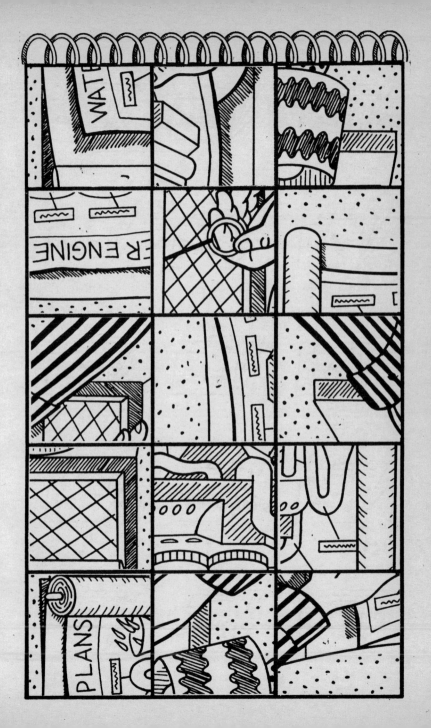

7

8

13

4

11

3

12

6

15

10

5

2

1

14

9

FINAL REPORT
TO THE CHIEF

Osgood had turned his company headquarters into a fortress. Only a mouse could have escaped from the shop, design lab, or office. But most mice can't carry blueprints.

McLever would have had the easiest time moving and hiding the blueprint. He knew Osgood best. Even without photographic memory, McLever could have taken the blueprint straight to Osgood's competitors. But he didn't. Why? He didn't have a reason to.

But Peck did. His motive? He wanted to embarrass Osgood. He was annoyed by Osgood's clutter. He didn't want to sell the blueprint to a competitor. He just wanted to scare the inventor into being a little neater. But because Peck needed to clean so perfectly, he laid his own trap and got caught.

The only place Peck had cleaned that didn't look perfect afterwards was one window in Osgood's office. Its windowshade was rolled up higher than the others. The blueprint was found rolled up inside the shade.

— CASE CLOSED —